Polar bear
at the
Christmas fair

Lesley Sims
Illustrated by David Semple

D1392627

"Hurray!" says Claire, the polar bear.
"Today's the Christmas fair."

"I'd like a ride," says Baby Bear and climbs into a car.

He drives around and up and down.

"Can we see Santa now?" asks Claire, walking past the rink.

SANTA

The three bears slide and glide on skates. "Oh my," says Gran.

Oh, wow!

"Let's see the market **first**," says Gran.
"Cheer up now. Don't be blue."

"I need some ribbons for my tree,
and twinkly tinsel too."

Gran takes her time to choose and pay.

"Now, Santa!" she declares.

Claire shoots ahead to show the way...

Time is short...
Presents to sort.
Had to go.
Ho ho ho!
Santa x

but just finds
empty chairs.

"He's gone?" says Gran.
"I'm sorry, Claire."

SANTA

Claire trudges home,
head down...

She sees a book.

Gran, come and look!

It's old and gold and brown.

She digs it up.
An elf runs up.

"It's Santa's list –
names, toys and games.
You are a sharp-eyed bear!"

"HO! HO! HO! Look out below."
A sleigh swoops through the air.

It's Santa!

Ho! Ho! Ho!
MERRY

CHRISTMAS!

Starting to read

Even before children start to recognize words, they can learn about the pleasures of reading. Encouraging a love of stories and a joy in language is the best place to start.

About phonics

When children learn to read in school, they are often taught to recognize words through phonics. This teaches them to identify the sounds of letters that are then put together to make words. An important first step is for children to hear rhymes, which help them to listen out for the sounds in words.

You can find out more about phonics on the Usborne website at **usborne.com/Phonics**

Phonics Readers

These rhyming books provide the perfect combination of fun and phonics. They are lively and entertaining with great story lines and quirky illustrations. They have the added bonus of focusing on certain sounds so in this story your child will soon identify the *air* sound, as in **fair** and **bear.** Look out, too, for rhymes such as **rink** – **think** and **declares** – **chairs**.

Reading with your child

If your child is reading a story to you, don't rush to correct mistakes, but be ready to prompt or guide if needed. Above all, give plenty of praise and encouragement.

Edited by Jenny Tyler
Designed by Sam Whibley

Reading consultants: Alison Kelly and Anne Washtell

First published in 2022 by Usborne Publishing Ltd., Usborne House, 83-85 Saffron Hill,
London EC1N 8RT, England. usborne.com Copyright © 2022 Usborne Publishing Ltd. The name
Usborne and the Balloon logo are Trade Marks of Usborne Publishing Ltd. All rights reserved.
No part of this publication may be reproduced, stored in a retrieval system, or transmitted
in any form or by any means without the prior permission of the publisher. UE.